D1237452

Boom Boom Mushroom #2

ABDO
Spotlight

DARK
HORSE
BOOKS

PopCap

Written by **PAUL TOBIN**

Art by **JACOB CHABOT**

Colors by **MATT J. RAINWATER**

Letters by **STEVE DUTRO**

Cover by **JACOB CHABOT**

President and Publisher **MIKE RICHARDSON**
Editor **PHILIP R. SIMON**
Assistant Editor **MEGAN WALKER**
Designer **BRENNAN THOME**
Digital Art Technician **CHRISTINA McKENZIE**

Special thanks to Leigh Beach, Gary Clay, A.J. Rathbun, Kristen Star, Jeremy Vanhoozer, and everyone at PopCap Games. Editorial thanks to Sal Paradise.

DarkHorse.com | PopCap.com

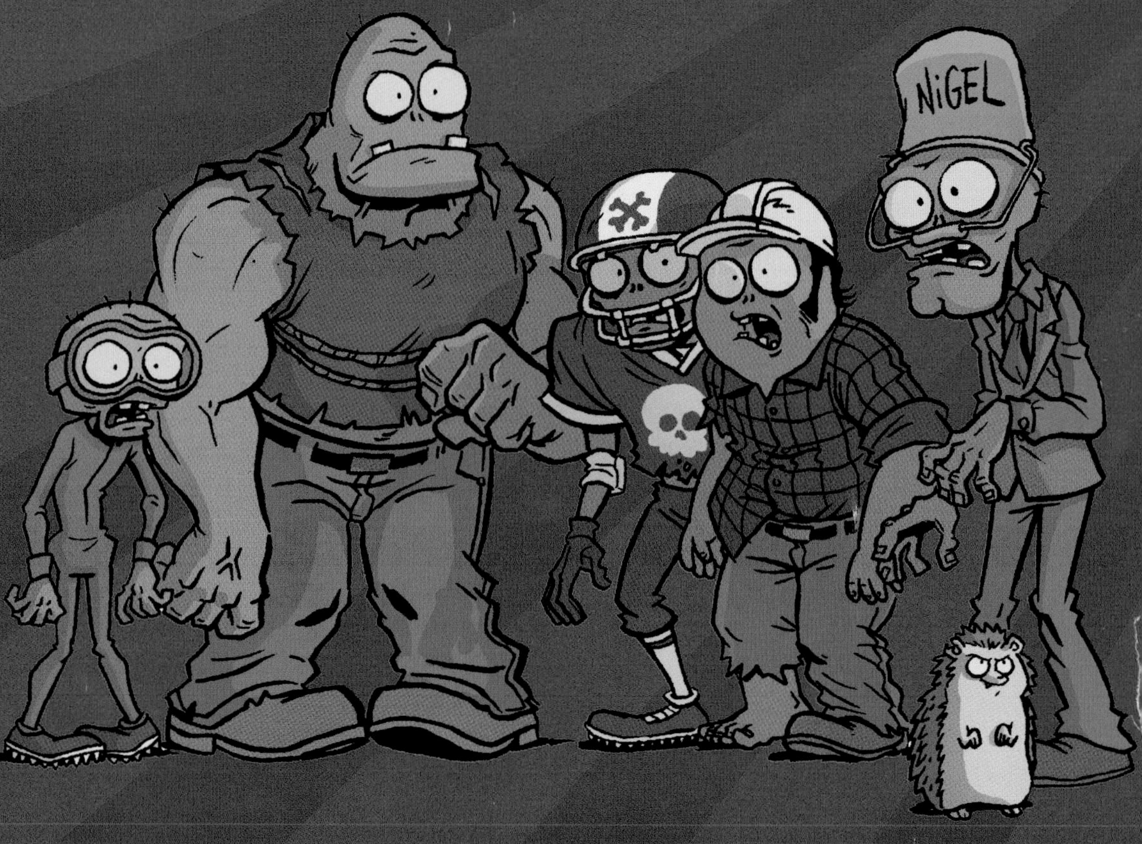
NiGEL

PLANTS VS. ZOMBIES

BOOM BOOM MUSHROOM #2

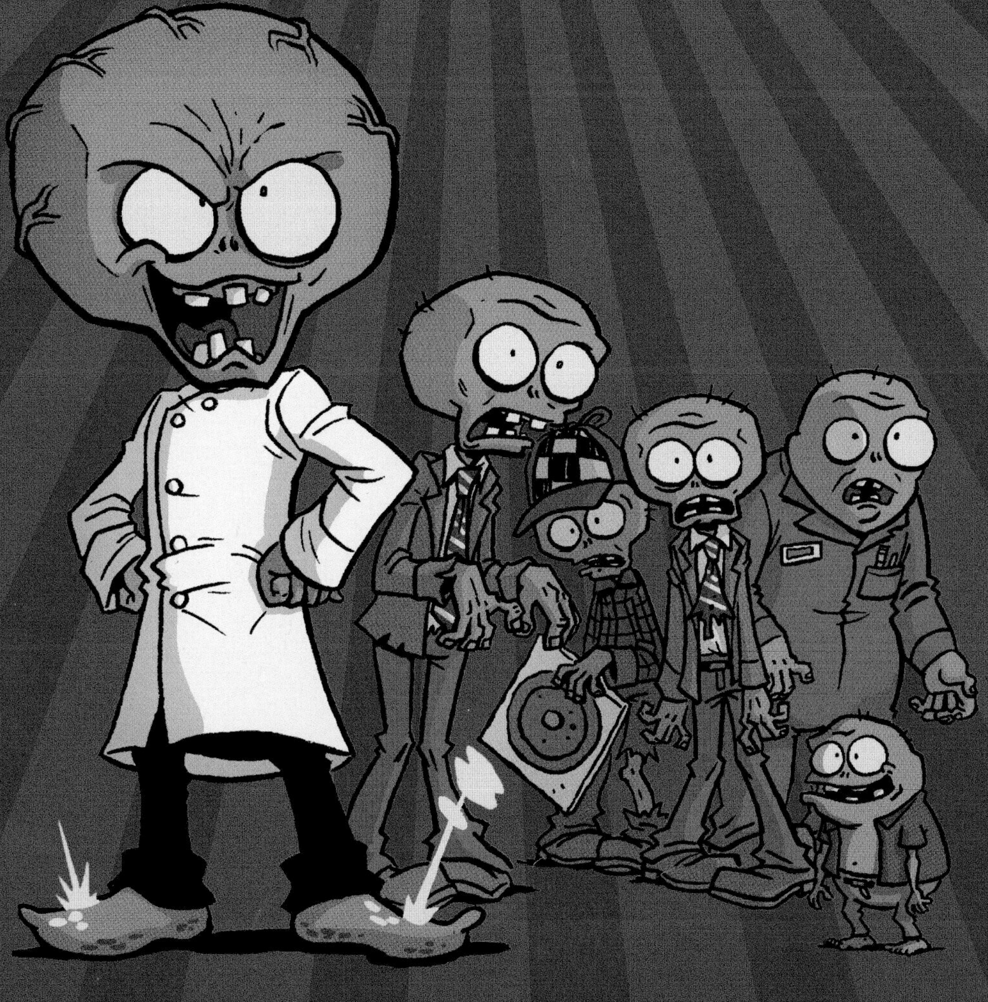

ABDOPUBLISHING.COM

Reinforced library bound edition published in 2018 by Spotlight, a division of ABDO,
PO Box 398166, Minneapolis, Minnesota 55439. Spotlight produces high-quality
reinforced library bound editions for schools and libraries.
Published by agreement with Dark Horse Comics.

Printed in the United States of America, North Mankato, Minnesota.
092017
012018

THIS BOOK CONTAINS
RECYCLED MATERIALS

Originally issued as Plants vs. Zombies #11: Boom Boom Mushroom Part 2
by Dark Horse Comics in 2016.

Plants vs. Zombies © 2016, 2017, 2018 Electronic Arts Inc. Plants vs. Zombies
and PopCap are trademarks of Electronic Arts Inc. All rights reserved.
Dark Horse Books® and the Dark Horse logo are registered trademarks of
Dark Horse Comics, Inc. All rights reserved.

PUBLISHER'S CATALOGING IN PUBLICATION DATA

Names: Tobin, Paul, author. | Chabot, Jacob ; Rainwater, Matthew J., illustrators.
Title: Boom Boom Mushroom / by Paul Tobin ; illustrated by Jacob Chabot and
   Matthew J. Rainwater.
Description: Minneapolis, MN : Spotlight, 2018 | Series: Plants vs. Zombies
Summary: When Patrice and Nate discover Zomboss's plan to raise an underground
   zombie army, they must race to find the rare Boom Boom Mushroom before
   Zomboss puts his plan in motion.
Identifiers: LCCN 2017941916 | ISBN 9781532141249 (v.1 : lib. bdg.) | ISBN
   9781532141256 (v.2 : lib. bdg.) | ISBN 9781532141263 (v.3 : lib. bdg.)
Subjects: LCSH: Plants--Juvenile fiction. | Zombies--Juvenile fiction. | Adventure and
   adventurers--Juvenile fiction. | Comic books, strips, etc.--Juvenile fiction. | Graphic
   novels--Juvenile fiction.
Classification: DDC 741.5--dc23
LC record available at http://lccn.loc.gov/2017941916

Spotlight

A Division of ABDO
abdopublishing.com

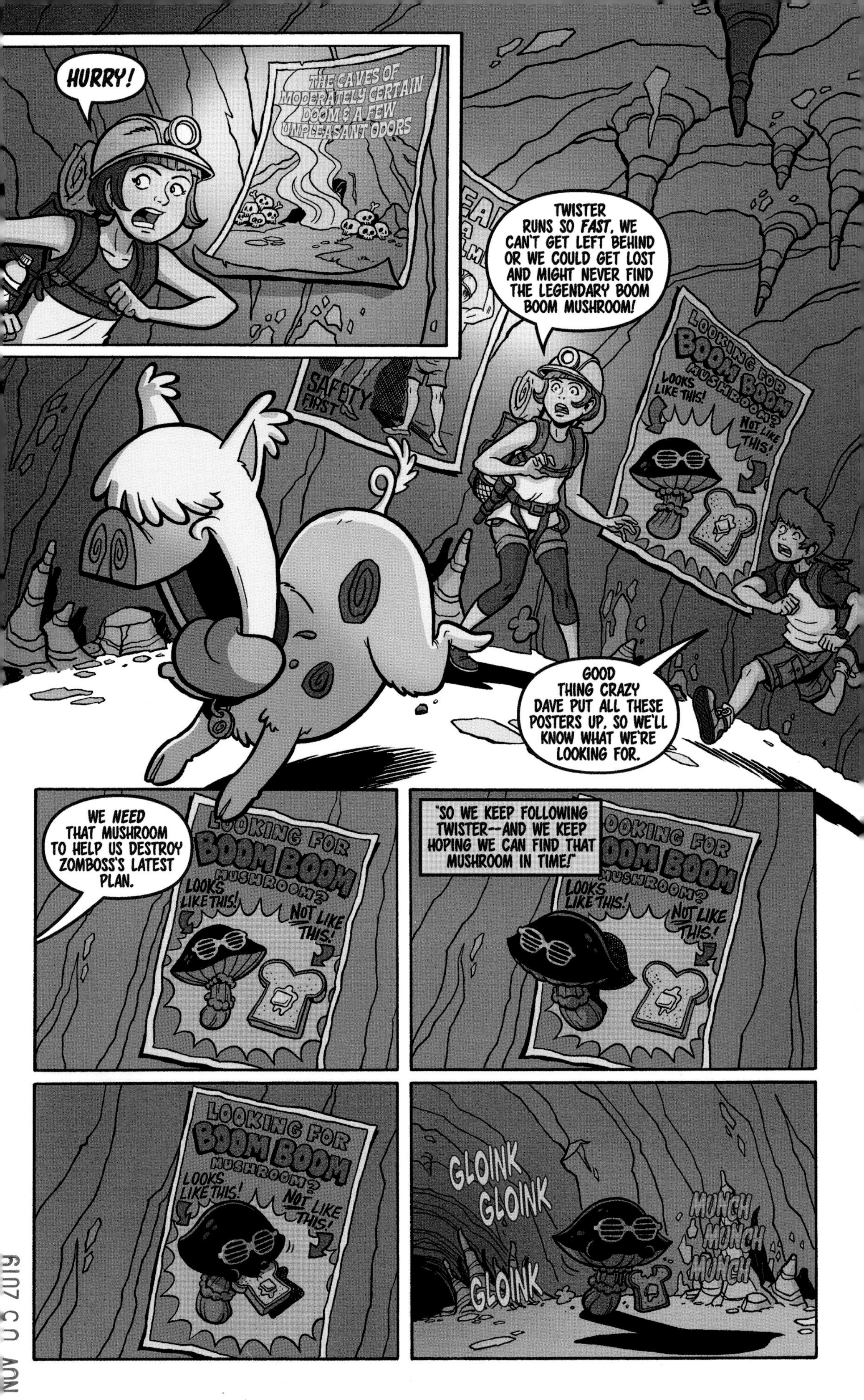
HURRY!
THE CAVES OF MODERATELY CERTAIN DOOM & A FEW UNPLEASANT ODORS
TWISTER RUNS SO FAST, WE CAN'T GET LEFT BEHIND OR WE COULD GET LOST AND MIGHT NEVER FIND THE LEGENDARY BOOM BOOM MUSHROOM!
SAFETY FIRST
LOOKING FOR BOOM BOOM MUSHROOM? LOOKS LIKE THIS! NOT LIKE THIS!
GOOD THING CRAZY DAVE PUT ALL THESE POSTERS UP, SO WE'LL KNOW WHAT WE'RE LOOKING FOR.
WE NEED THAT MUSHROOM TO HELP US DESTROY ZOMBOSS'S LATEST PLAN.
LOOKING FOR BOOM BOOM MUSHROOM? LOOKS LIKE THIS! NOT LIKE THIS!
"SO WE KEEP FOLLOWING TWISTER--AND WE KEEP HOPING WE CAN FIND THAT MUSHROOM IN TIME!"
LOOKING FOR BOOM BOOM MUSHROOM? LOOKS LIKE THIS! NOT LIKE THIS!
LOOKING FOR BOOM BOOM MUSHROOM? LOOKS LIKE THIS! NOT LIKE THIS!
GLOINK
GLOINK
GLOINK
MUNCH
MUNCH
MUNCH

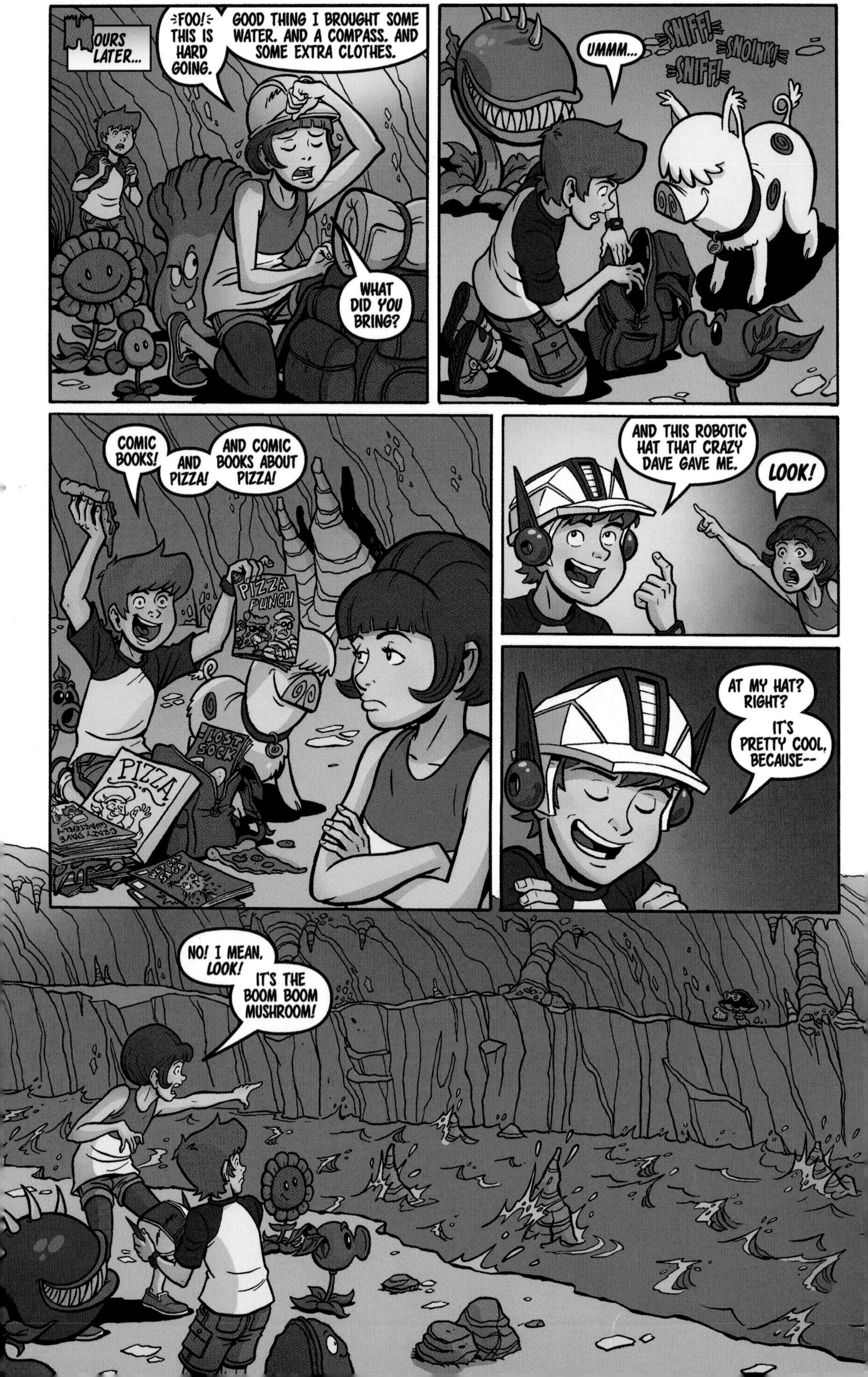
HOURS LATER...
FOO! THIS IS HARD GOING.
GOOD THING I BROUGHT SOME WATER. AND A COMPASS. AND SOME EXTRA CLOTHES.
WHAT DID YOU BRING?
UMMM...
SNIFF!
SNOINK!
SNIFF!
COMIC BOOKS!
AND PIZZA!
AND COMIC BOOKS ABOUT PIZZA!
PIZZA PUNCH
LOST SOCK
PIZZA
WET CAT SAGA
AND THIS ROBOTIC HAT THAT CRAZY DAVE GAVE ME.
LOOK!
AT MY HAT? RIGHT?
IT'S PRETTY COOL, BECAUSE--
NO! I MEAN, LOOK!
IT'S THE BOOM BOOM MUSHROOM!

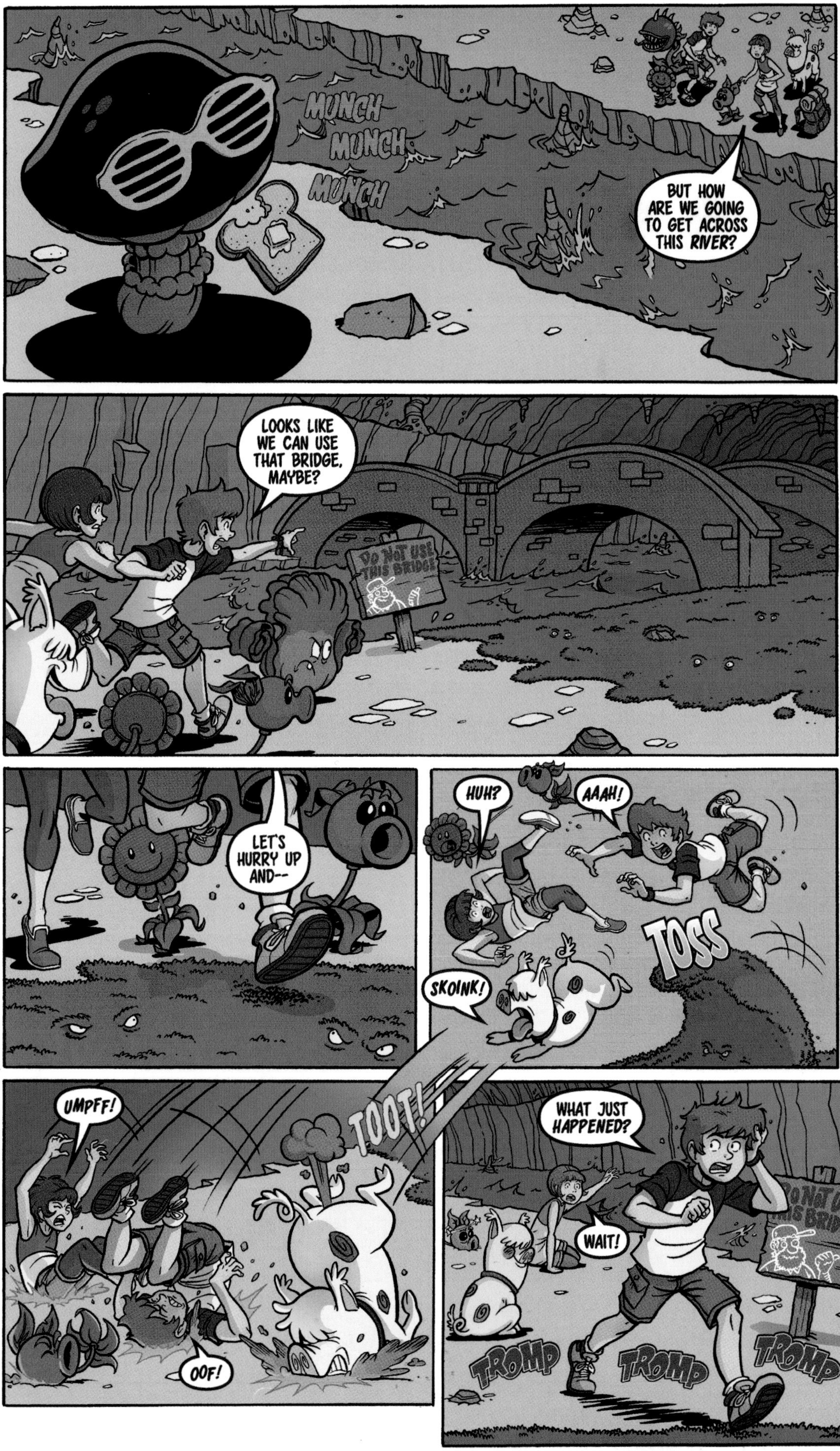
MUNCH
MUNCH
MUNCH
BUT HOW ARE WE GOING TO GET ACROSS THIS RIVER?
LOOKS LIKE WE CAN USE THAT BRIDGE, MAYBE?
DO NOT USE THIS BRIDGE
LET'S HURRY UP AND--
HUH?
AAAH!
TOSS
SKOINK!
UMPFF!
TOOT!
OOF!
WHAT JUST HAPPENED?
WAIT!
DO NOT USE THIS BRIDGE
TROMP
TROMP
TROMP

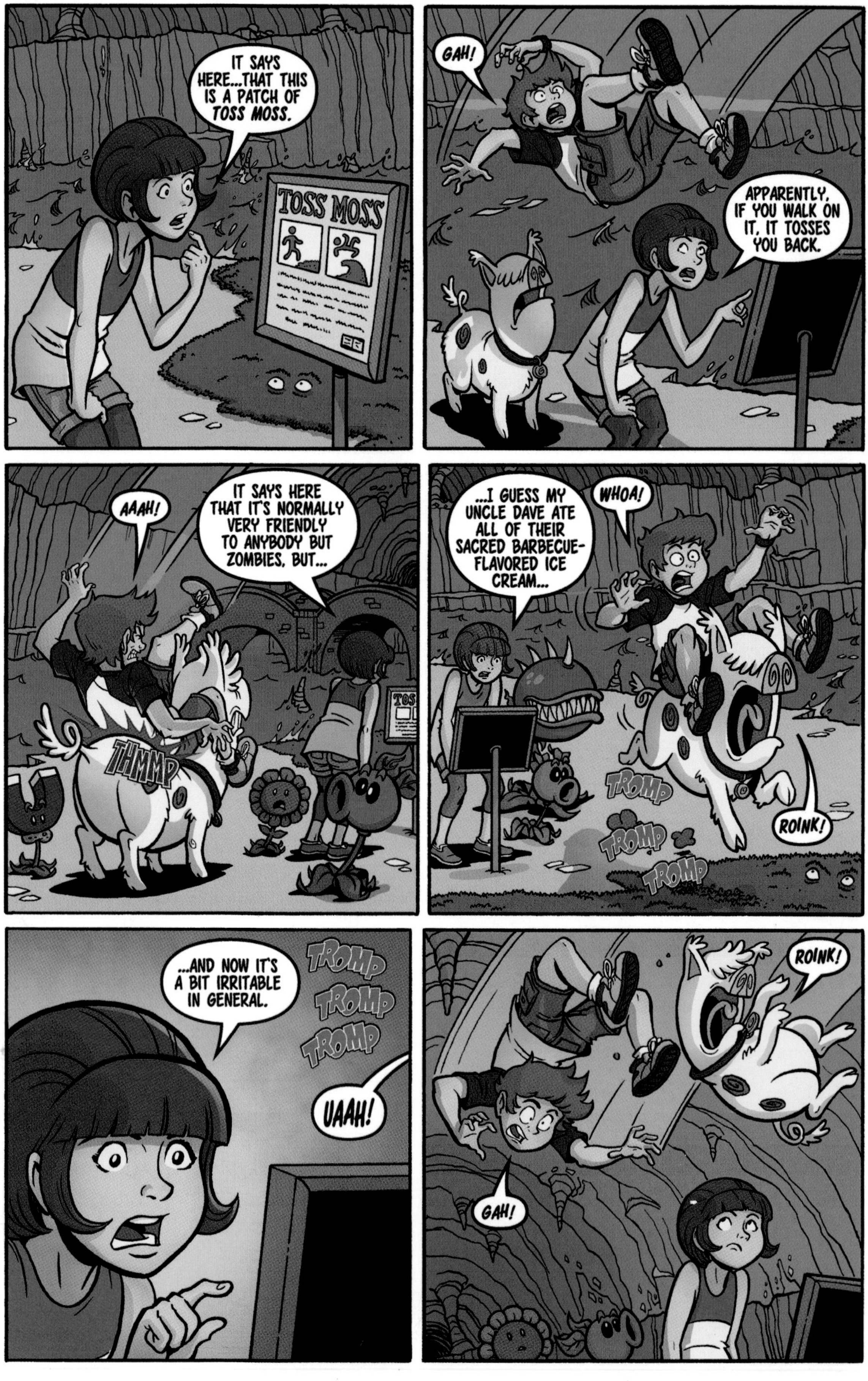
IT SAYS HERE...THAT THIS IS A PATCH OF TOSS MOSS.
TOSS MOSS
GAH!
APPARENTLY, IF YOU WALK ON IT, IT TOSSES YOU BACK.
AAAH!
IT SAYS HERE THAT IT'S NORMALLY VERY FRIENDLY TO ANYBODY BUT ZOMBIES, BUT...
THMMP
TOS
...I GUESS MY UNCLE DAVE ATE ALL OF THEIR SACRED BARBECUE-FLAVORED ICE CREAM...
WHOA!
TROMP
TROMP
TROMP
ROINK!
...AND NOW IT'S A BIT IRRITABLE IN GENERAL.
TROMP
TROMP
TROMP
UAAH!
ROINK!
GAH!

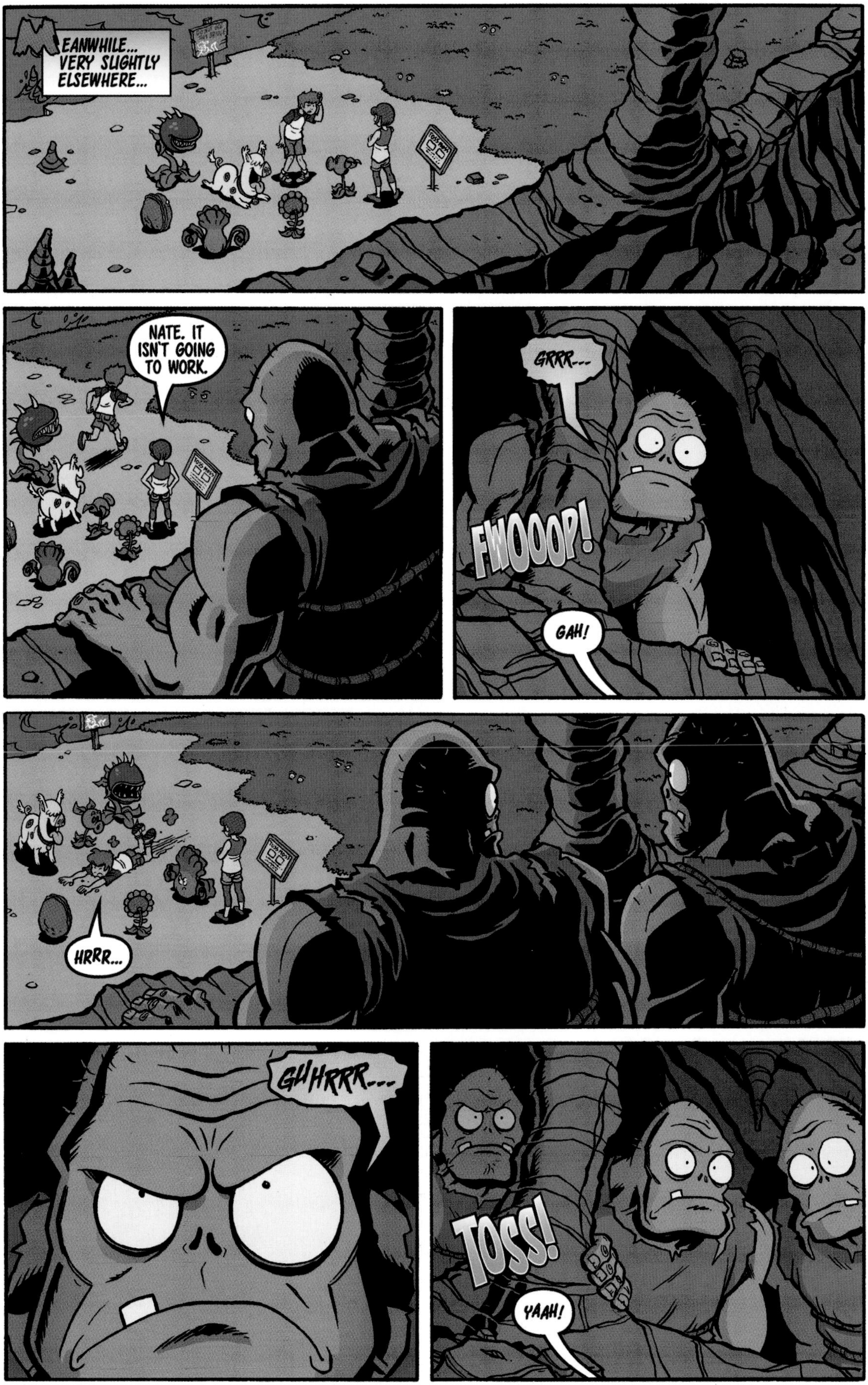
MEANWHILE... VERY SLIGHTLY ELSEWHERE...
NATE. IT ISN'T GOING TO WORK.
GRRR...
FWOOOP!
GAH!
HRRR...
GUHRRR...
TOSS!
YAAH!

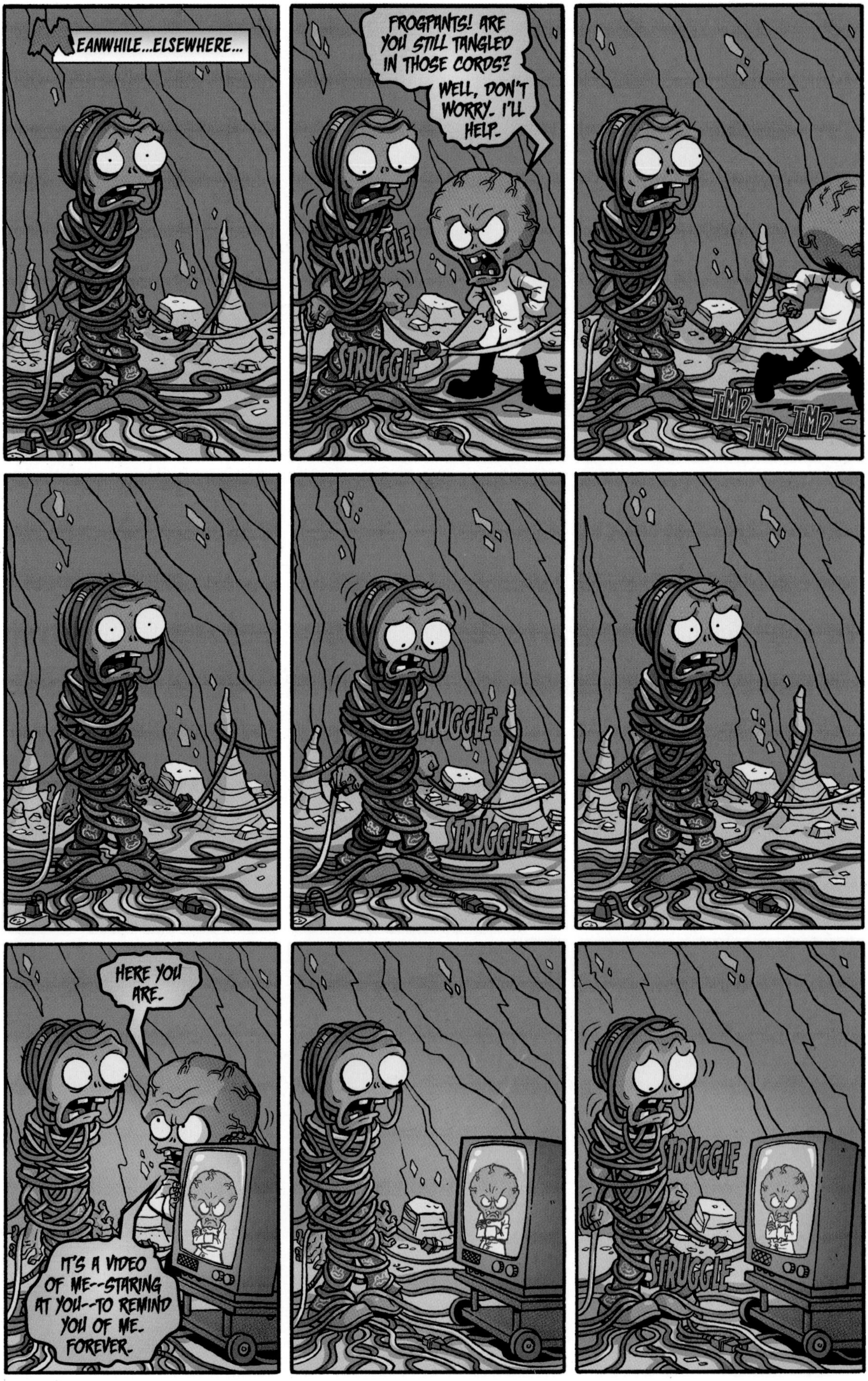
MEANWHILE...ELSEWHERE...
FROGPANTS! ARE YOU STILL TANGLED IN THOSE CORDS?
WELL, DON'T WORRY. I'LL HELP.
STRUGGLE
STRUGGLE
TMP TMP TMP
STRUGGLE
STRUGGLE
HERE YOU ARE.
IT'S A VIDEO OF ME--STARING AT YOU--TO REMIND YOU OF ME. FOREVER.
STRUGGLE
STRUGGLE

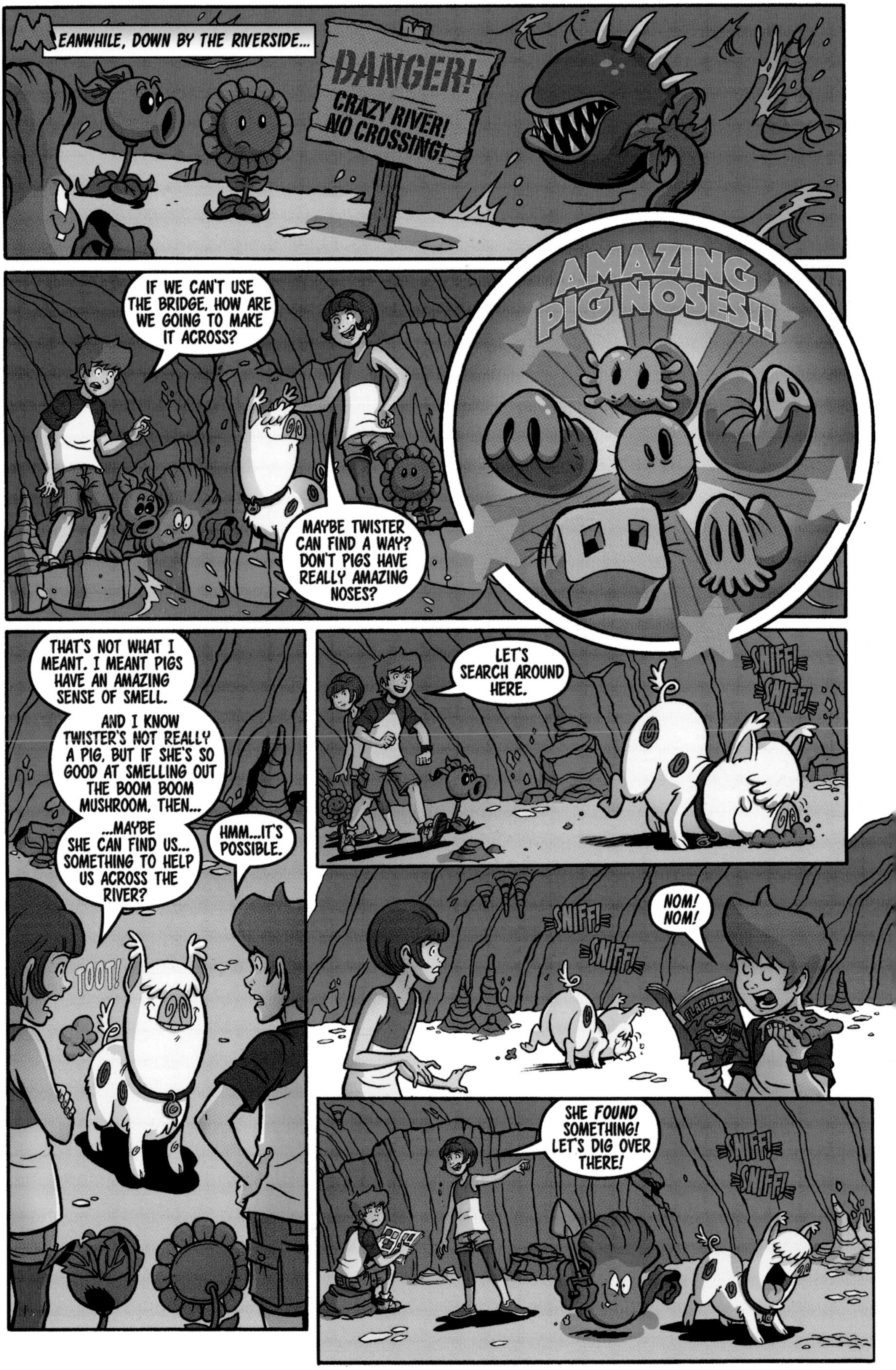
MEANWHILE, DOWN BY THE RIVERSIDE...
DANGER!
CRAZY RIVER! NO CROSSING!
IF WE CAN'T USE THE BRIDGE, HOW ARE WE GOING TO MAKE IT ACROSS?
MAYBE TWISTER CAN FIND A WAY? DON'T PIGS HAVE REALLY AMAZING NOSES?
AMAZING PIG NOSES!!
THAT'S NOT WHAT I MEANT. I MEANT PIGS HAVE AN AMAZING SENSE OF SMELL.
AND I KNOW TWISTER'S NOT REALLY A PIG, BUT IF SHE'S SO GOOD AT SMELLING OUT THE BOOM BOOM MUSHROOM, THEN...
...MAYBE SHE CAN FIND US... SOMETHING TO HELP US ACROSS THE RIVER?
HMM...IT'S POSSIBLE.
TOOT!
LET'S SEARCH AROUND HERE.
SNIFF!
SNIFF!
SNIFF!
SNIFF!
NOM! NOM!
SHE FOUND SOMETHING! LET'S DIG OVER THERE!
SNIFF!
SNIFF!

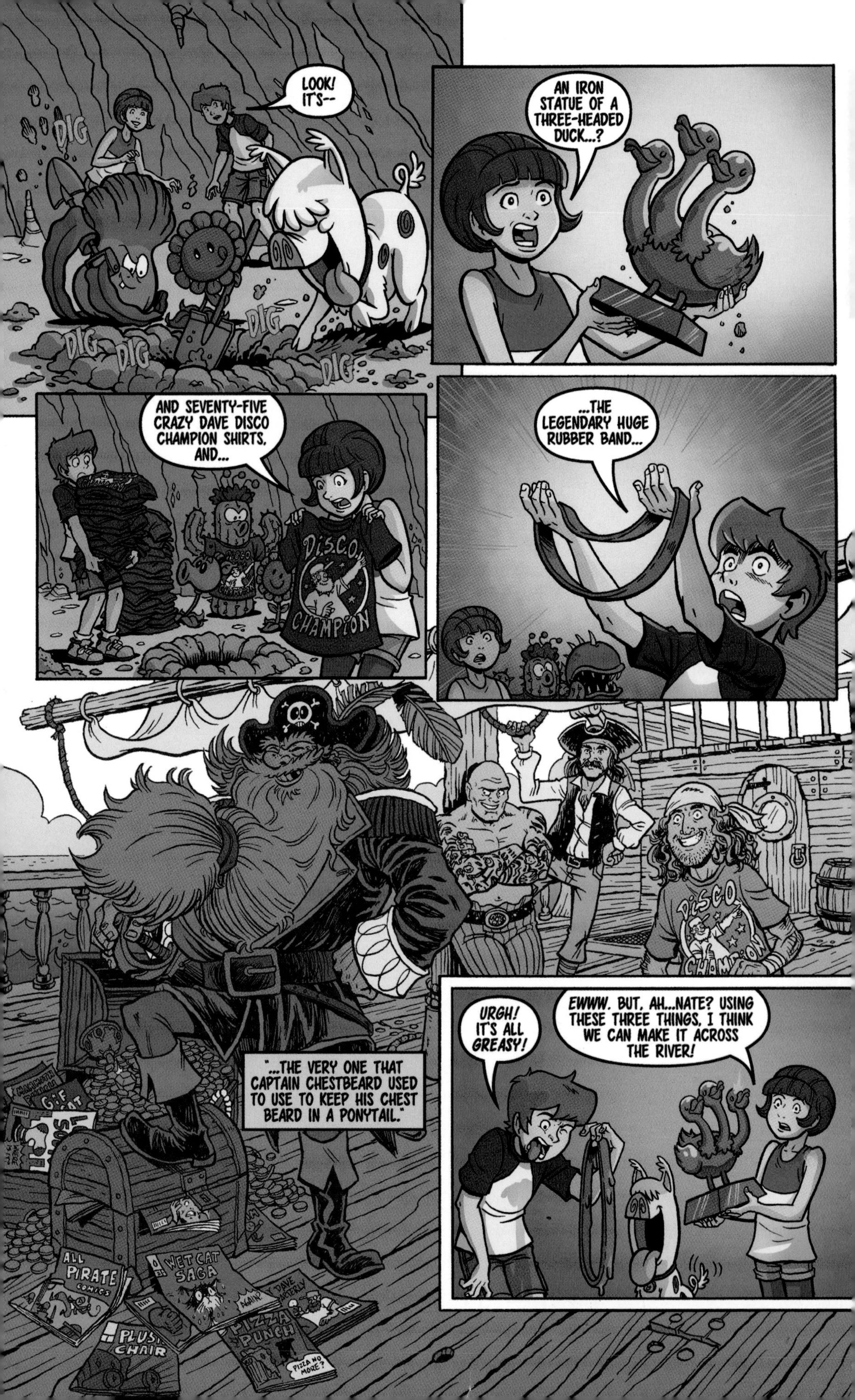
DIG
DIG
DIG
DIG
DIG
LOOK! IT'S--
AN IRON STATUE OF A THREE-HEADED DUCK...?
AND SEVENTY-FIVE CRAZY DAVE DISCO CHAMPION SHIRTS, AND...
DISCO CHAMPION
...THE LEGENDARY HUGE RUBBER BAND...
"...THE VERY ONE THAT CAPTAIN CHESTBEARD USED TO USE TO KEEP HIS CHEST BEARD IN A PONYTAIL."
DISCO CHAMPION
ALL PIRATE COMICS
WET CAT SAGA
PIZZA PUNCH
PLUSH CHAIR
URGH! IT'S ALL GREASY!
EWWW. BUT, AH...NATE? USING THESE THREE THINGS, I THINK WE CAN MAKE IT ACROSS THE RIVER!

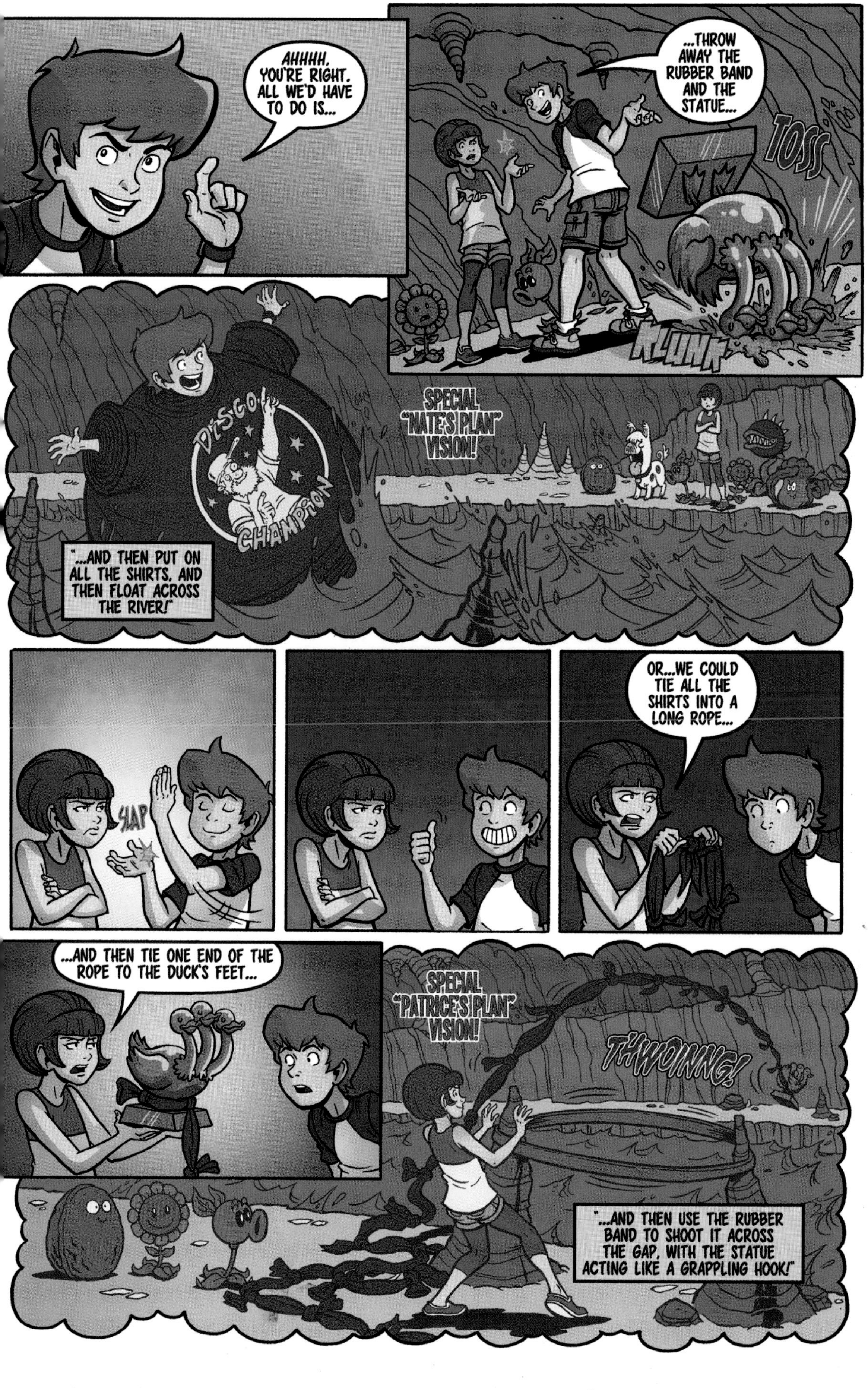
AHHHH, YOU'RE RIGHT. ALL WE'D HAVE TO DO IS...
...THROW AWAY THE RUBBER BAND AND THE STATUE...
TOSS
KLUNK
SPECIAL "NATE'S PLAN" VISION!
DISCO CHAMPION
"...AND THEN PUT ON ALL THE SHIRTS, AND THEN FLOAT ACROSS THE RIVER!"
SLAP
OR...WE COULD TIE ALL THE SHIRTS INTO A LONG ROPE...
...AND THEN TIE ONE END OF THE ROPE TO THE DUCK'S FEET...
SPECIAL "PATRICE'S PLAN" VISION!
THWOINNG!
"...AND THEN USE THE RUBBER BAND TO SHOOT IT ACROSS THE GAP, WITH THE STATUE ACTING LIKE A GRAPPLING HOOK!"

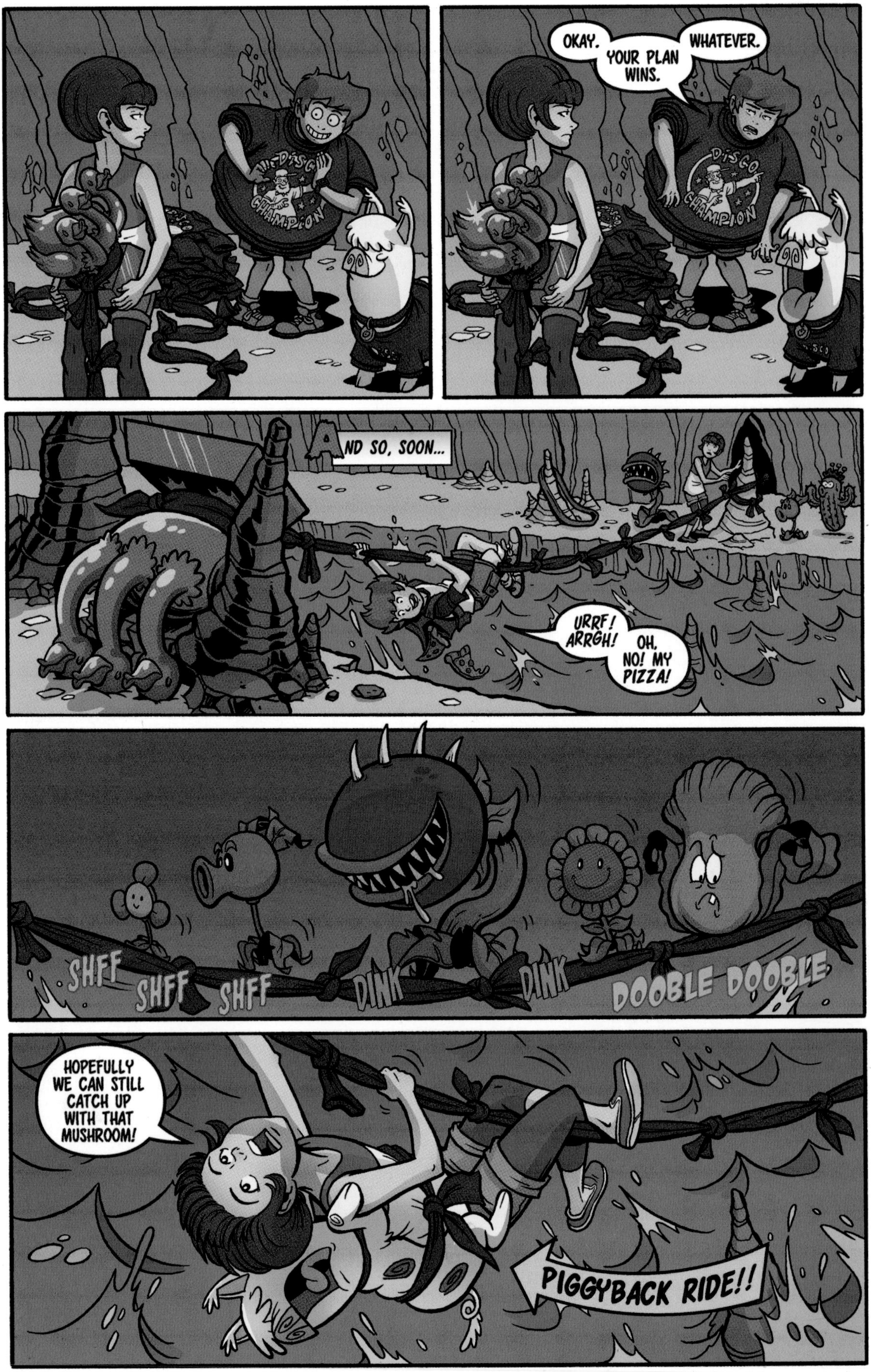
OKAY.
YOUR PLAN WINS.
WHATEVER.
AND SO, SOON...
URRF! ARRGH!
OH, NO! MY PIZZA!
SHFF
SHFF
SHFF
DINK
DINK
DOOBLE DOOBLE
HOPEFULLY WE CAN STILL CATCH UP WITH THAT MUSHROOM!
PIGGYBACK RIDE!!

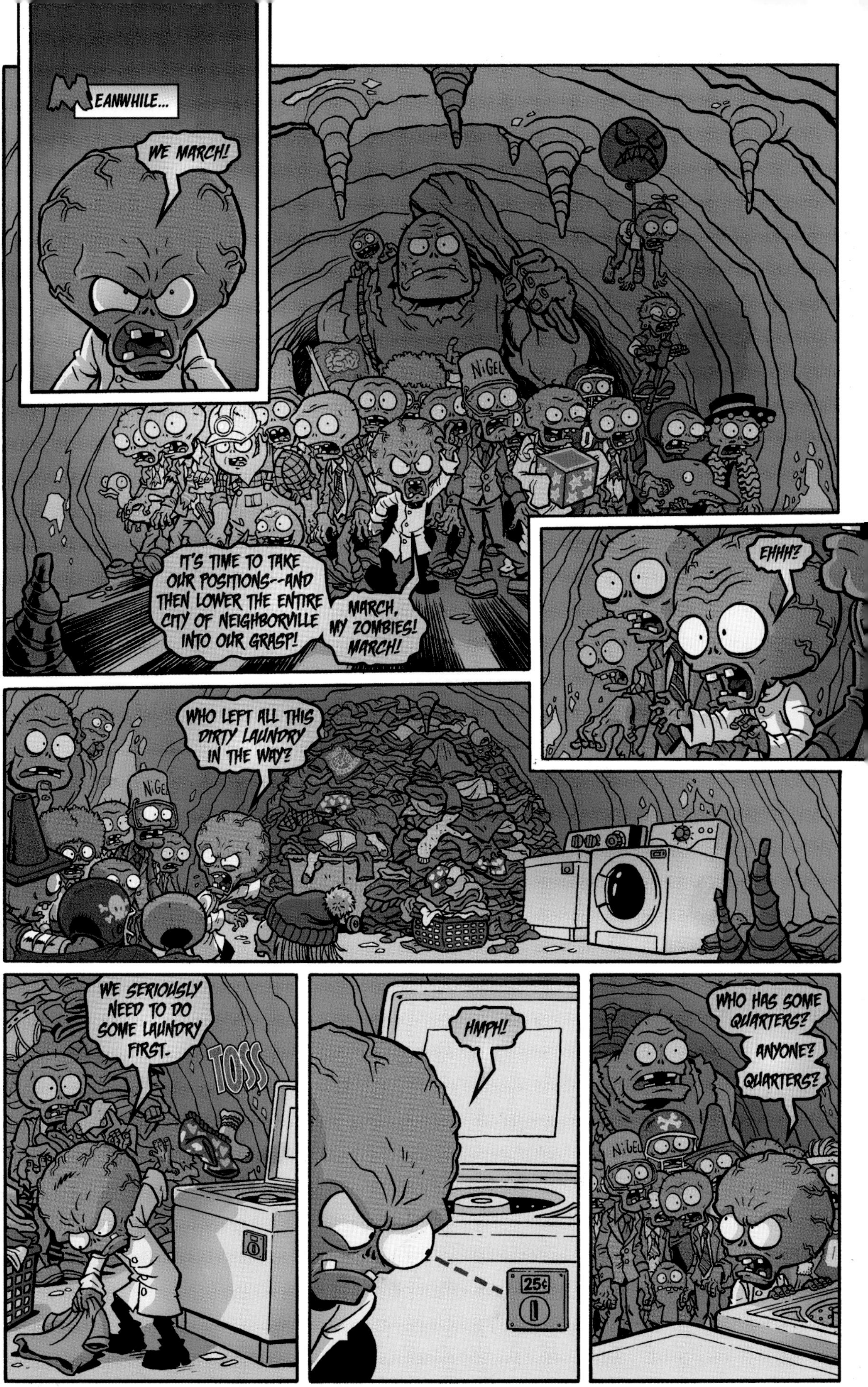
MEANWHILE...
WE MARCH!
N-GEL
IT'S TIME TO TAKE OUR POSITIONS--AND THEN LOWER THE ENTIRE CITY OF NEIGHBORVILLE INTO OUR GRASP!
MARCH, MY ZOMBIES! MARCH!
EHHH?
WHO LEFT ALL THIS DIRTY LAUNDRY IN THE WAY?
WE SERIOUSLY NEED TO DO SOME LAUNDRY FIRST.
TOSS
HMPH!
25¢
WHO HAS SOME QUARTERS?
ANYONE?
QUARTERS?

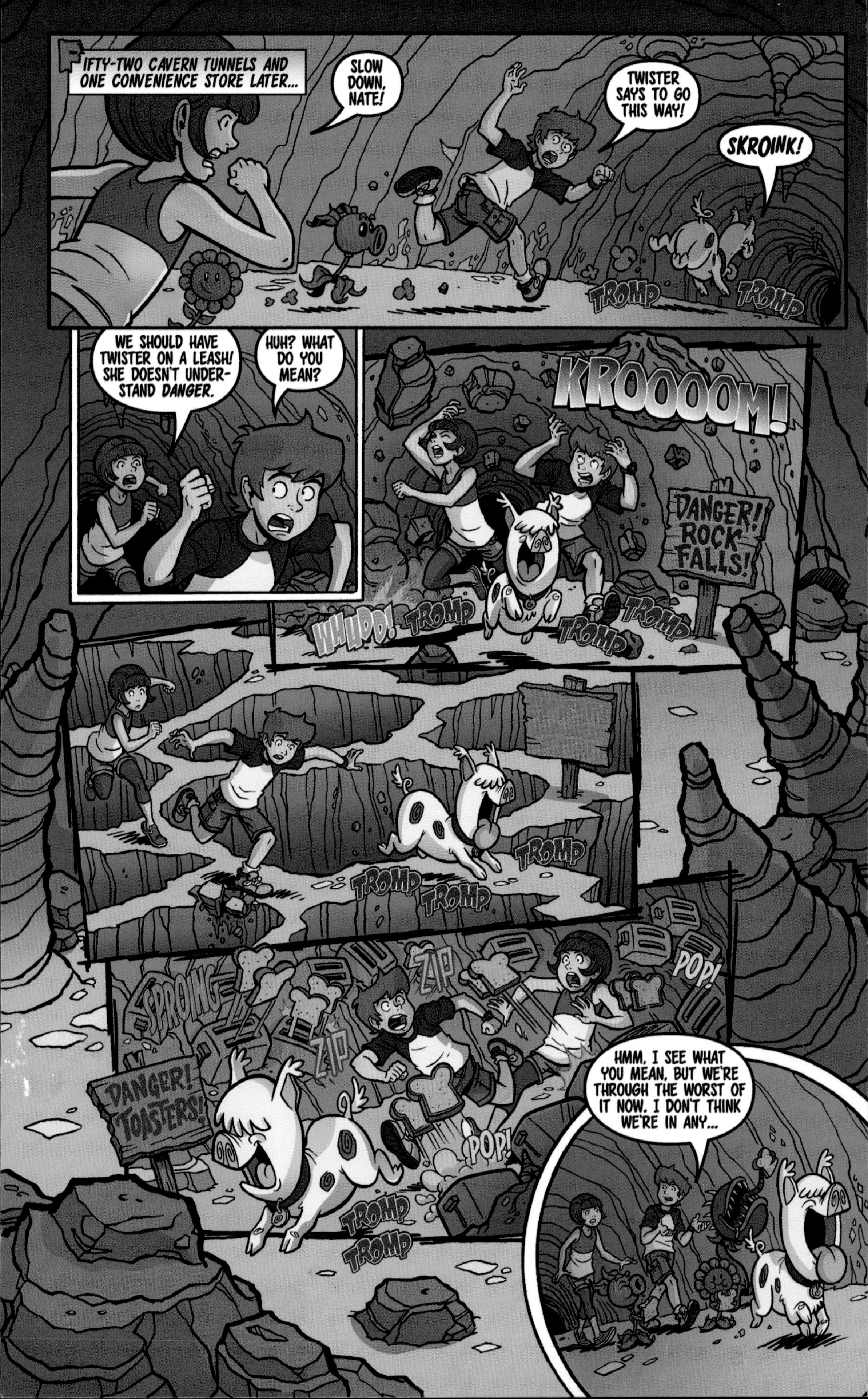
FIFTY-TWO CAVERN TUNNELS AND ONE CONVENIENCE STORE LATER...
SLOW DOWN, NATE!
TWISTER SAYS TO GO THIS WAY!
SKROINK!
TROMP
TROMP
WE SHOULD HAVE TWISTER ON A LEASH! SHE DOESN'T UNDER-STAND DANGER.
HUH? WHAT DO YOU MEAN?
KROOOOOM!
DANGER! ROCK FALLS!
WHUDD!
TROMP
TROMP
TROMP
TROMP
TROMP
TROMP
SPROING
ZIP
POP!
ZIP
DANGER! TOASTERS!
POP!
TROMP
TROMP
HMM, I SEE WHAT YOU MEAN, BUT WE'RE THROUGH THE WORST OF IT NOW. I DON'T THINK WE'RE IN ANY...

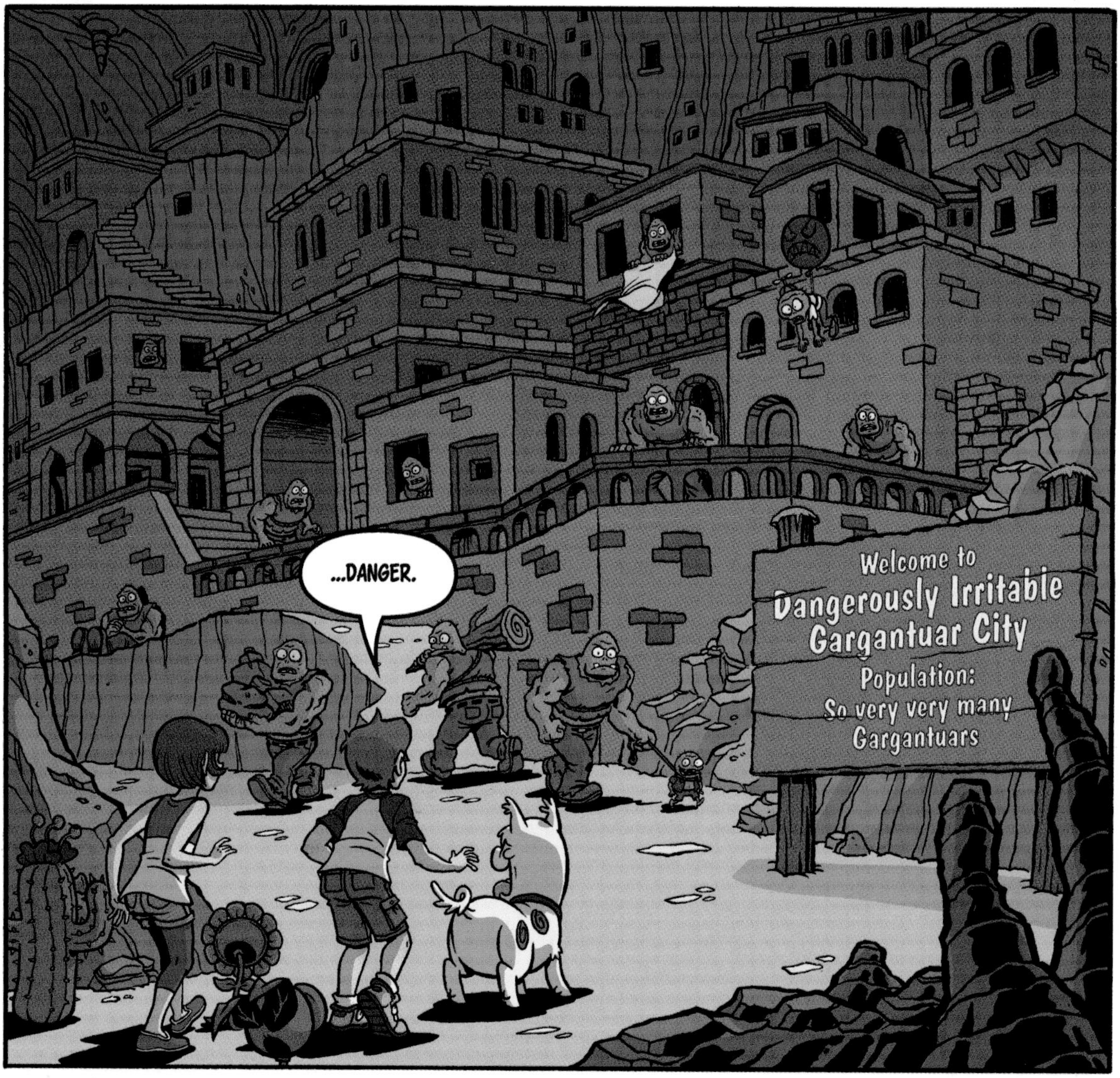
...DANGER.
Welcome to
Dangerously Irritable
Gargantuar City
Population:
So very very many
Gargantuars

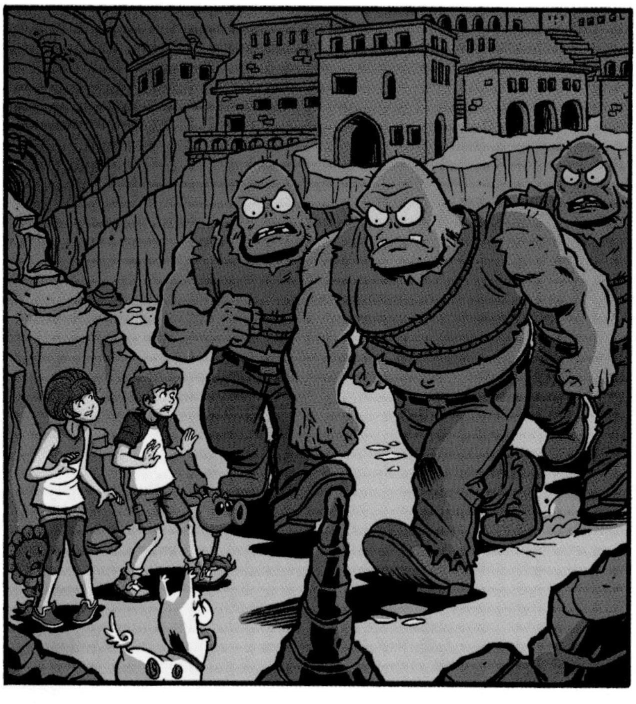

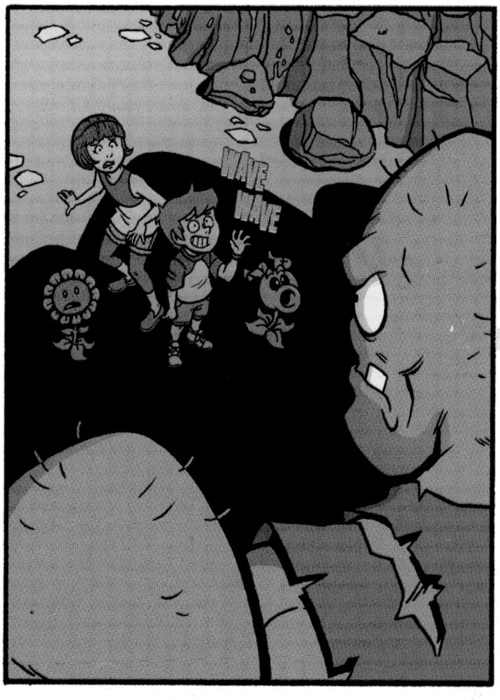
WAVE
WAVE

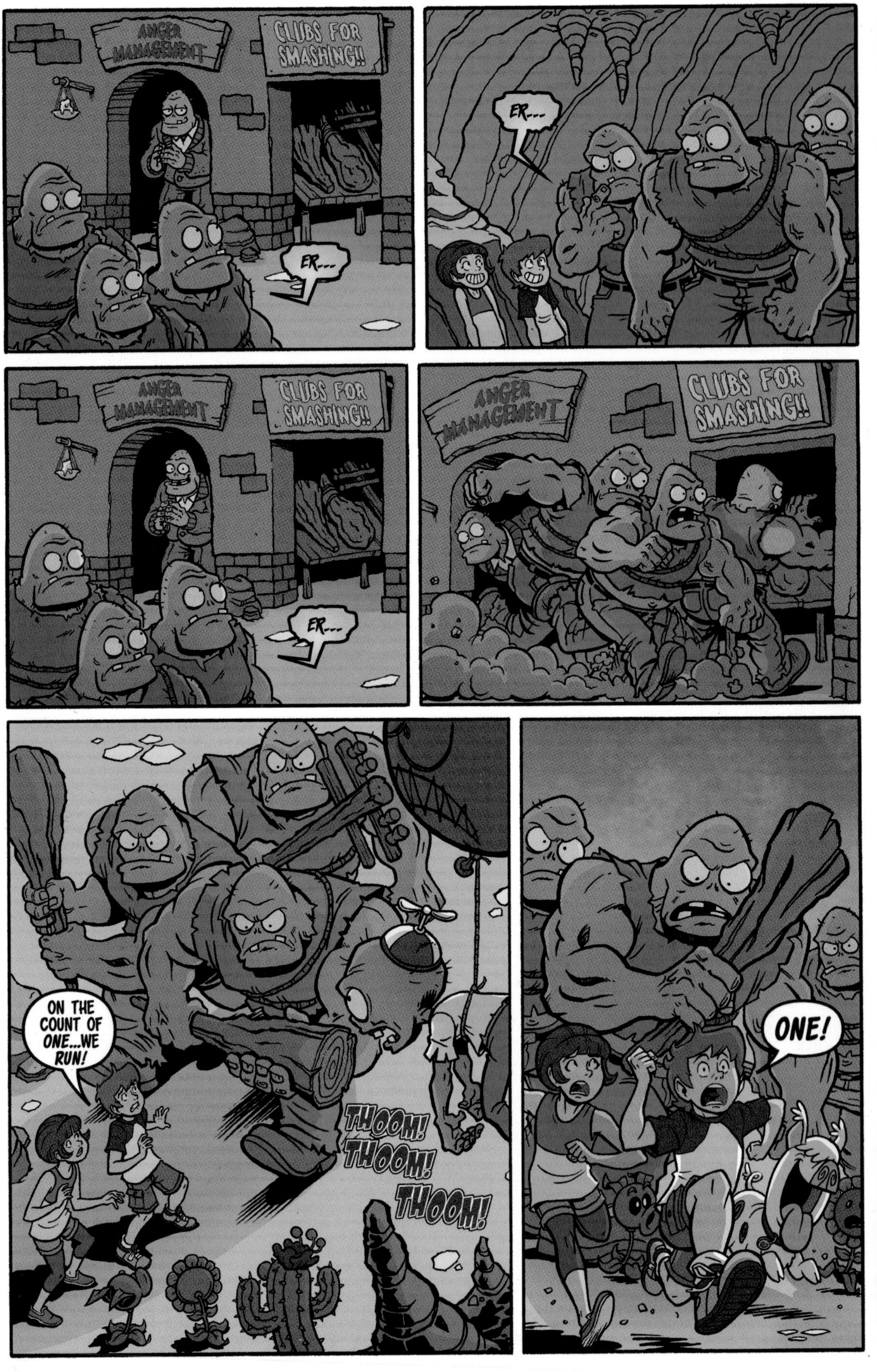
ANGER MANAGEMENT
CLUBS FOR SMASHING!!
ER...
ER...
ANGER MANAGEMENT
CLUBS FOR SMASHING!!
ER...
ANGER MANAGEMENT
CLUBS FOR SMASHING!!
ON THE COUNT OF ONE...WE RUN!
THOOM! THOOM! THOOM!
ONE!

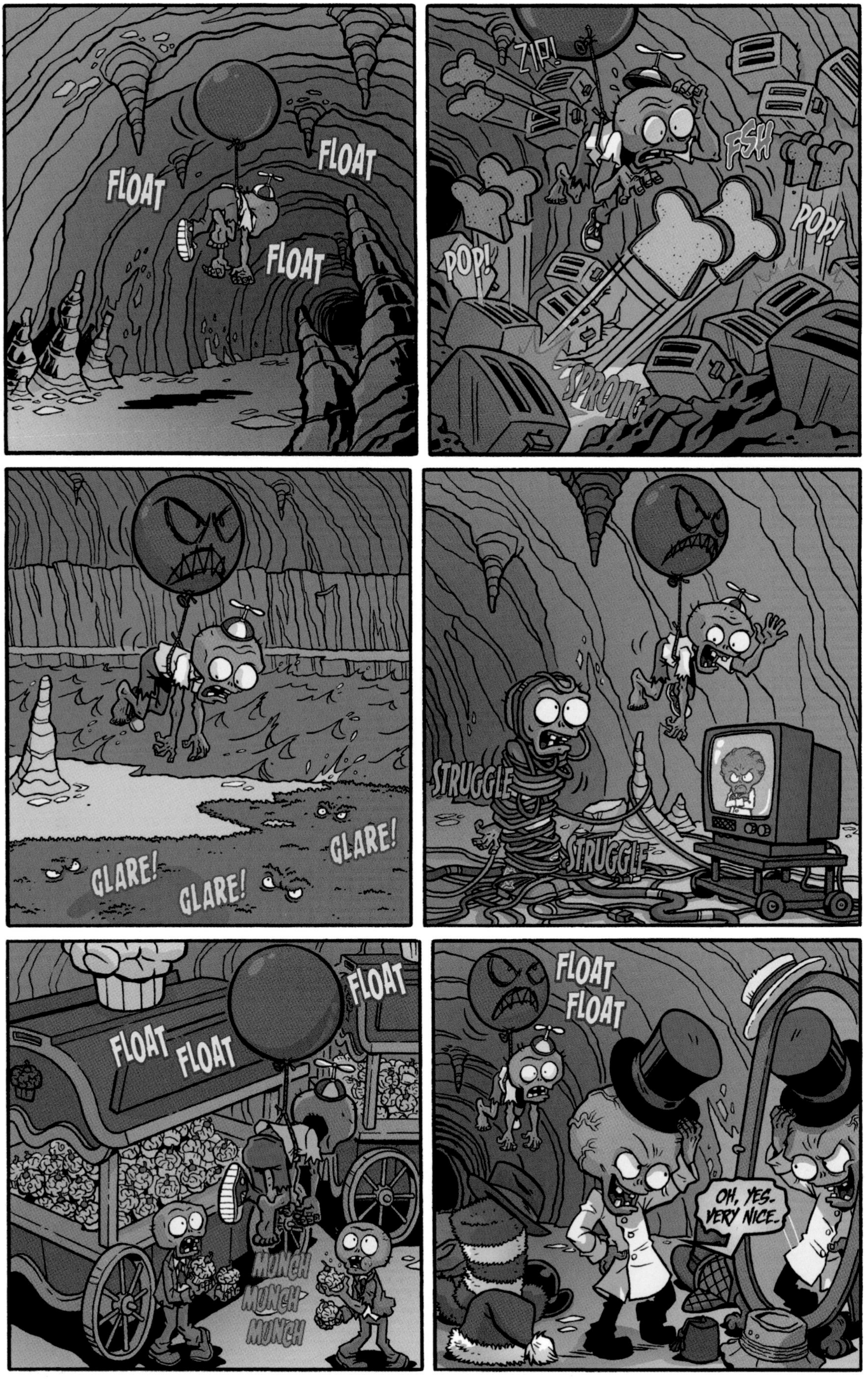
FLOAT
FLOAT
FLOAT
ZIP!
FSH
POP!
POP!
SPROING
GLARE!
GLARE!
GLARE!
STRUGGLE
STRUGGLE
FLOAT
FLOAT
FLOAT
MUNCH
MUNCH
MUNCH
FLOAT
FLOAT
OH, YES. VERY NICE.

BRAINS. BRAAAAINS!

HUH? THOSE KIDS? EVEN HERE IN MY UNDERGROUND LAIR?

I'LL TAKE CARE OF THIS! I'LL SEND MY VERY BEST ZOMBIE!

HMM...

HMM...HMM...HMM...

HMM...

MR. STUBBINS! I HAVE A JOB FOR YOU!

HERE, LET ME WHISPER THIS EVIL PLAN INTO YOUR EAR.

WHISPER WHISPER WHISPER WHISPER WHISPER WHISPER WHISPER WHISPER WHISPER WHISPER WHISPER WHISPER WHISPER WHISPER WHISPER WHISPER WHISPER

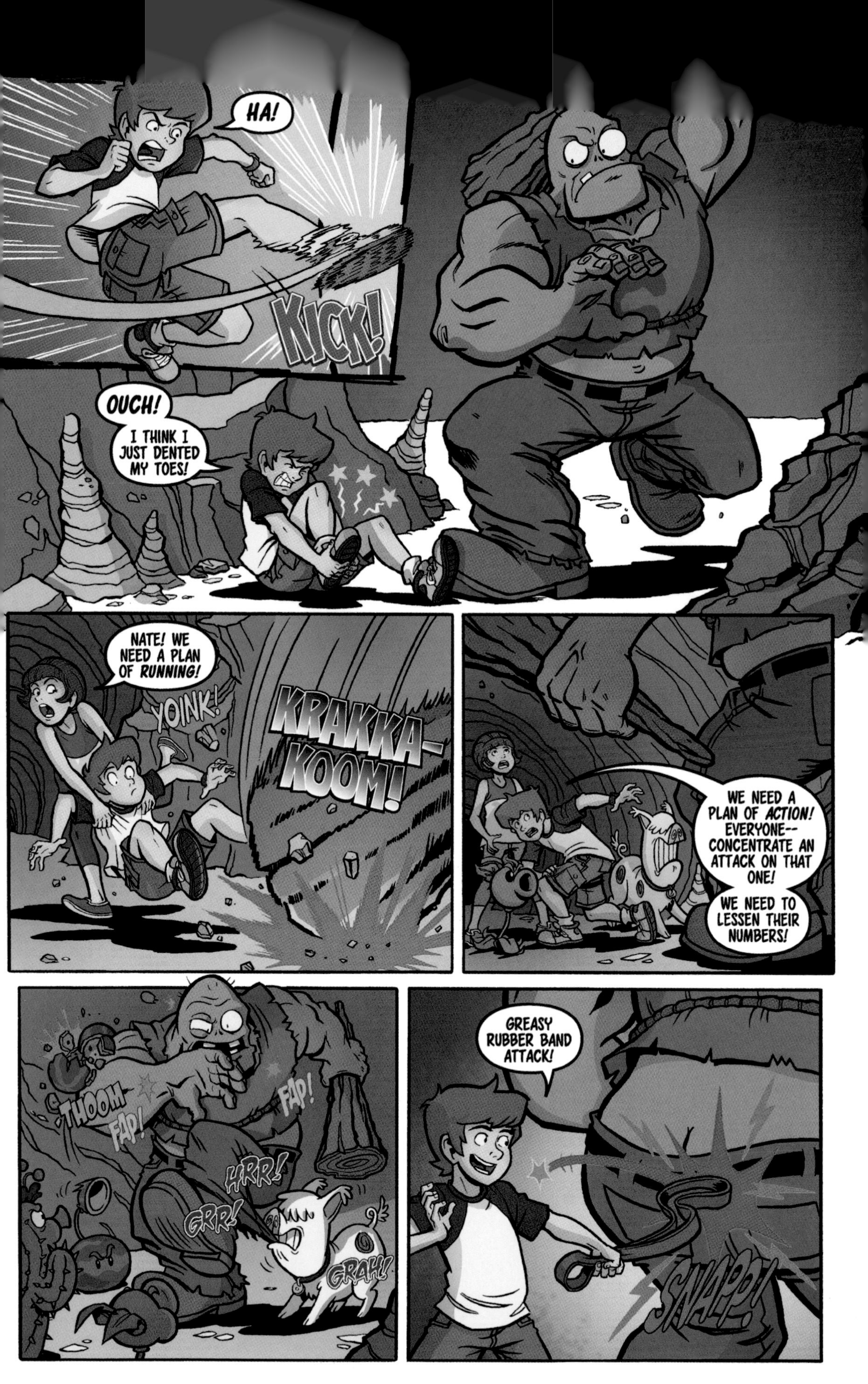

HA!
KICK!
OUCH!
I THINK I JUST DENTED MY TOES!
NATE! WE NEED A PLAN OF *RUNNING!*
YOINK!
KRAKKA-KOOM!
WE NEED A PLAN OF *ACTION!* EVERYONE--CONCENTRATE AN ATTACK ON THAT ONE!
WE NEED TO LESSEN THEIR NUMBERS!
THOOM
FAP!
FAP!
HRR!
GRR!
GRAH!
GREASY RUBBER BAND ATTACK!
SNAP!

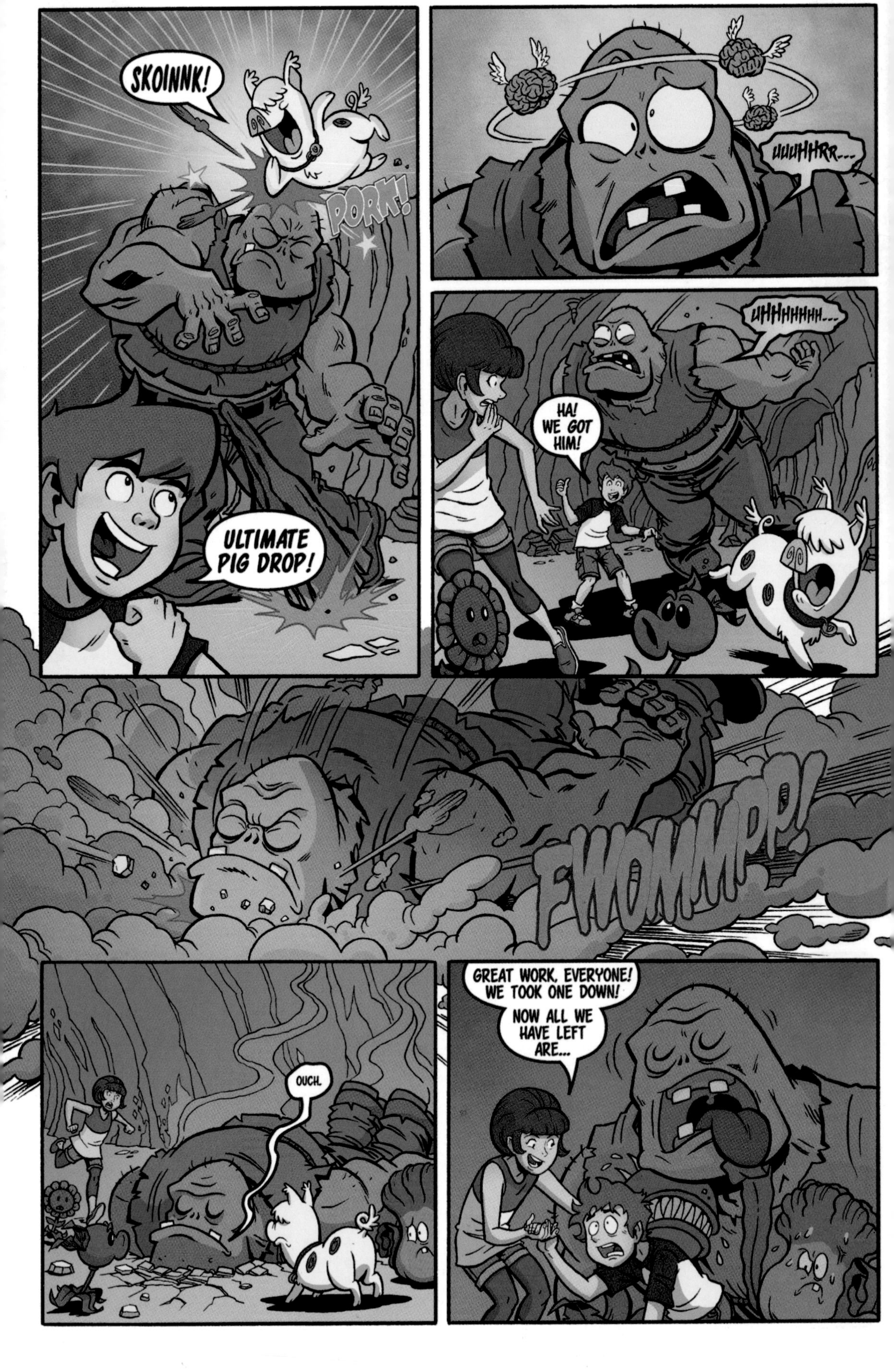
SKOINNK!
PORK!
ULTIMATE PIG DROP!
UUUHHRR...
UHHHHHHH...
HA! WE GOT HIM!
FWOMMPP!
OUCH.
GREAT WORK, EVERYONE! WE TOOK ONE DOWN!
NOW ALL WE HAVE LEFT ARE...

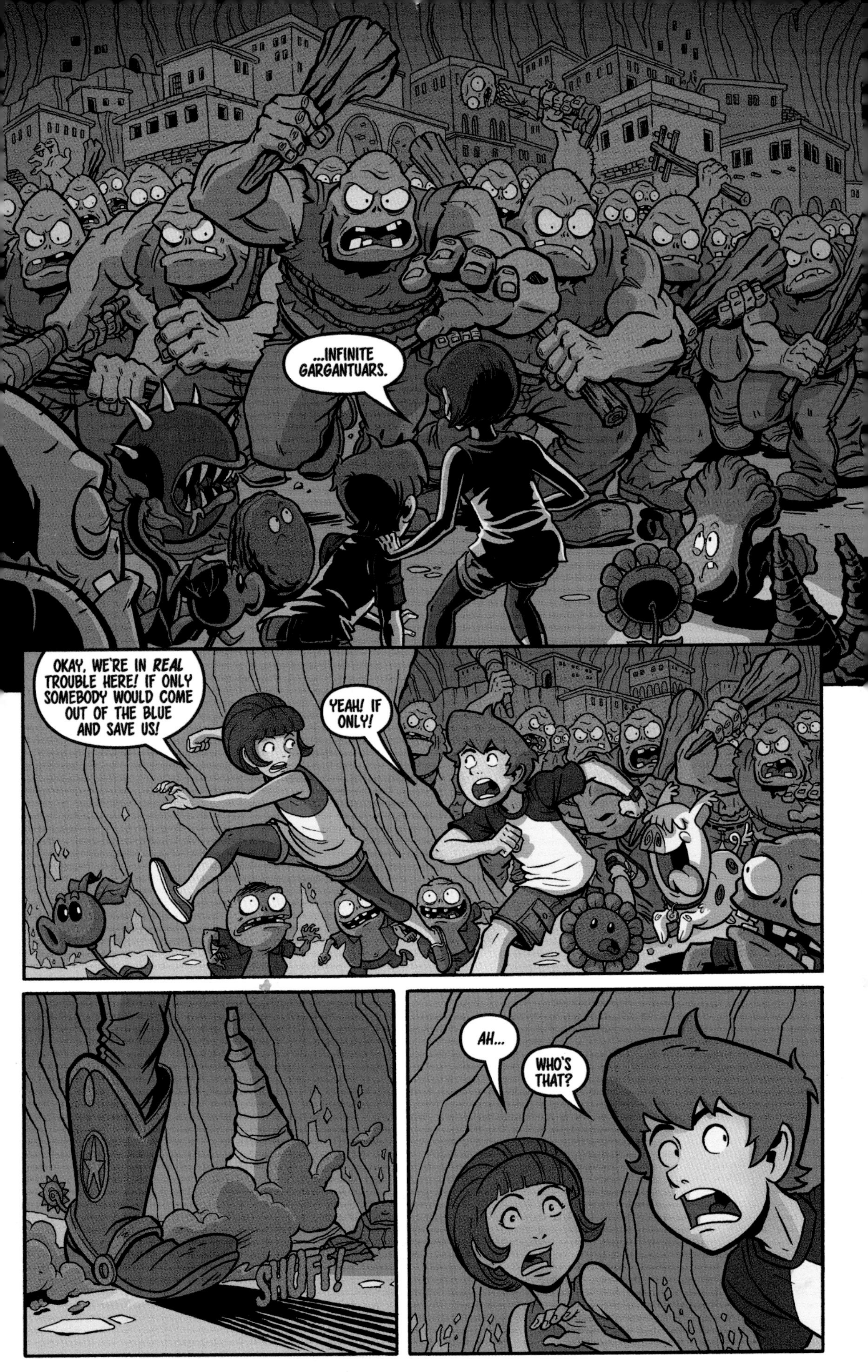
...INFINITE GARGANTUARS.
OKAY, WE'RE IN REAL TROUBLE HERE! IF ONLY SOMEBODY WOULD COME OUT OF THE BLUE AND SAVE US!
YEAH! IF ONLY!
SHUFF!
AH...
WHO'S THAT?

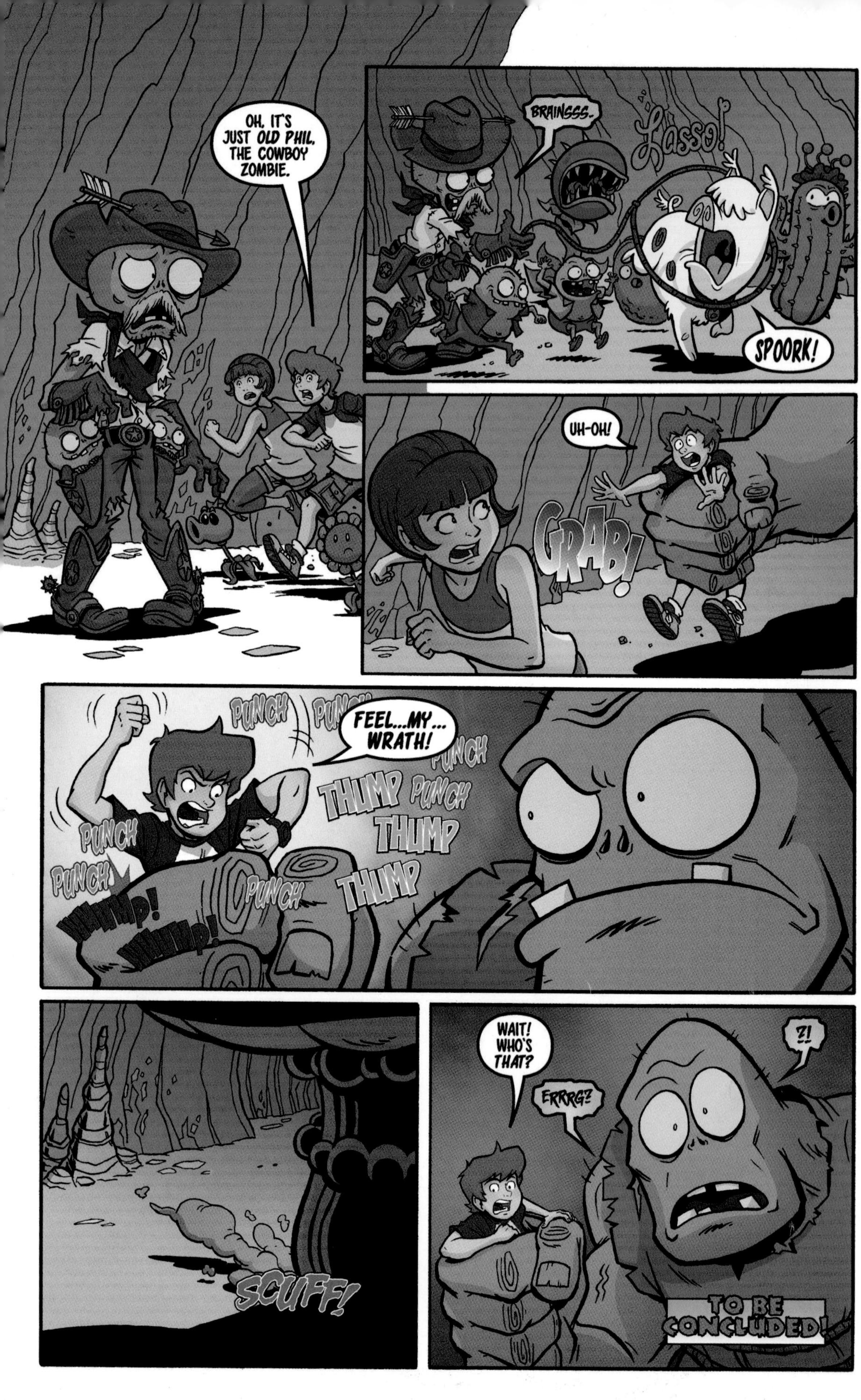
OH, IT'S JUST OLD PHIL, THE COWBOY ZOMBIE.
BRAINSSS.
Lasso!
SPOORK!
UH-OH!
GRAB!
PUNCH
PUNCH
FEEL...MY... WRATH!
PUNCH
THUMP
PUNCH
THUMP
PUNCH
PUNCH
PUNCH
THUMP
WHUMP!
WHUMP!
SCUFF!
WAIT! WHO'S THAT?
ERRRG?
?!
TO BE CONCLUDED!